Isabella—Her Story

Isabella—Her Story

(A Dachshund's Tale)

Wm. Thomas Brown

VANTAGE PRESS
New York

This is a work of fiction. Any similarity between the
names and characters in this book and any real persons,
living or dead, is purely coincidental.

FIRST EDITION

Published by Vantage Press, Inc.
419 Park Ave. South, New York, NY 10016

Manufactured in the United States of America
ISBN: 978-0-533-15938-3

Library of Congress Catalog Card No.: 2007908718

0 9 8 7 6 5 4 3 2 1

Isabella—Her Story

Isabella

The Early Years

In January 1995 I was born to a black mother in the corner of a small room with only one overhead light and virtually no furniture. I learned later in my youth that Mother was not totally black, but it seemed so at the time. And it made sense since I was black, and my two triplet sisters were also black. I've always felt lucky about being the middle triplet, because most folks aren't born with both a younger and an older sibling. Since Mother had little time to figure out names for us such as Daisy or Maggie and the like, she took the easy way out and named me "Two" since I was the second born. Likewise, my older sister was called "One," and the last born, she called "Three." For a long time I wondered if my name was spelled "two," "to," or "too." Mother told me not to worry about it since it was meant to sound like "ooo" as in "cute," which I was.

Mother was always a good provider. There was always plenty of food for the three of us, and while Mother never ate her meals with us in the early years, she always seemed well nourished herself. That Mother of ours was a strict disciplinarian. From the beginning she always insisted upon good manners. We were never allowed to fuss or fight over our food or our proper places while eating.

We were able to see our father only a few times when

we grew older, and we never knew him at all. He was a real mystery, and even though we asked questions about him many times, Mother always more or less dodged the question and said that that was a matter between the two of them. One time when "Three" and I ragged her for an answer she surrendered a little and said, "You'll know sometime. You may even get to meet him one day." Then she smiled that little enigmatic smile of hers that she did so well and continued by telling us, "Your daddy is a real champion, a real 'hot dog' of a guy." But we were practically grown before we ever saw him, and I, personally, was not impressed. "One" one day suggested that perhaps they saw each other on the sly, and he might not even know that the three of us existed. After awhile, as we grew older, the three of us gave up pestering Mother and let the matter drop. Obviously, we realized we were a one-parent family, and even if we had no father, we had a mother who loved us and protected us.

I have already pointed out that Mother was a good provider even as a single parent. We always had plenty to eat, and we didn't really need much in the way of clothes. We were always warm enough, but even though we were warm, our noses were always runny and cold. My nose always seemed colder than my two sisters', and even though we fussed about it, we eventually learned to live with it, especially after Mother told us that cold noses run in the family. Mother's nose was always cold too.

We didn't know what Mother did for a living. I thought that she might be a waitress in a nearby restaurant with flexible hours that suited her. Any time that the three of us were hungry, Mother was always there with enough food to satisfy us, and generally once she had fed us, she would leave again . . . but she was always able to run home when we needed her. I thought that perhaps she owned the restaurant. "Three" thought she might be a nurse of some kind, because she always knew exactly what to do if one of us didn't feel well. That didn't happen often, but when it did, she was always there. Mother was mysterious about her job, and wouldn't discuss it. "One" had her own ideas about the matter, but said they were too awful to share with us, her younger sisters, and that she tried not to think about it. "One" had an evil mind.

A New Beginning

One evening after dinner, the four of were lounging around in our room when Mother called us together for what she referred to as our "evening lessons." These lessons didn't happen every day, only when Mother felt like it, but they became more frequent as the three of us grew older. I liked this time together for it made us feel close like a family.

She taught us:

1. Always be nice to everyone you meet, even if you don't want to, and don't really like them.
2. Always be grateful for your food, even if it becomes boring because it is the same thing every day.
3. Always be happy, and even if you're not, act that way.
4. Always do what is right even if you don't want to.

Mother was always right in so many ways, and even as I have grown up I always try to follow her advice. (Of course, I don't always succeed.)

That evening when we were all relaxing, Mother told us a lot more about ourselves. We learned that in addition to our dad's being a "real champion," Mother herself was also a champion as were our grandparents on both sides of our family as far back as she had been able to trace our ancestry. We also learned that we were of German blood, and that in ancient times, our ancestors had hunted for a living. They were Badger hunters. The words "Badger hunters" grabbed my attention and triggered something deep in my mind. I conjured up all kinds of questions.

What is a Badger? What kind of champions? Boxers? Wrestlers? Beauty Queens? And I wondered just what Mother was about to tell us.

Well, we didn't have to wait very long for the big news . . . the big blow, that is. Mother told us that we are all Dachshunds!!! We are dogs!!! I screamed, "Oh no, no!" "Three" went to the corner and cried, while "One" just sat there with a dumb look on her face. Then Mother said, "Now, see here, it is wonderful being a dog today in America. Leading a dog's life is not what it once was, especially if you are a Dachshund. Tomorrow I will teach you how to do cute things which will nearly always get you anything you want in life. And once you've learned how to be 'cute,' I'll let you meet Daryl who owns this place. He thinks he owns us, but of course we know better. We Dachshunds are never really owned by anyone."

That evening as we three snuggled down to bed, my head was spinning with all kinds of questions. I was especially curious about what "cute" meant. "Three" was still whimpering. "One," always playing the part of older sister said, "Now listen up, you guys and shape up. Do you realize that dog spelled backwards spells God? And that is good. There wouldn't be anything without God. We're probably in on the ground floor of something big." "Three" quit whimpering. "One" rolled over and went to sleep after finding Mother and having a small late-night snack. I spent most of the night contemplating my cold nose and trying to figure out how "One" had become so educated about God.

"Master Daryl" and the Kennel

I could hardly wait until the next morning to meet "Master Daryl." That is what everyone called him. But let me hasten to point out the lesson that Mother had taught us time after time, and that is that Dachshunds NEVER have masters. If someone happens to think that he or she is our master, we'll let him think it, but we Dachshunds know better, and that is just the way it is.

We went to the front of the main house and there was Daryl sitting on the front porch in a swing. He was a handsome dude, as dudes go, tallish with black hair like mine without the brown markings around his nose. He picked up the three of us, and held us in his lap, and petted us on our heads. I liked him from the beginning, and since I couldn't pet him back, I licked his hands and arms. Daryl put "One" and "Three" back on the floor next to Mother, and held me next to his face, still stroking me on the head and rubbing my tummy. I liked this very much, and to return his friendship, I gave him a slurpy lick across his lips. This is how I learned to kiss. Daryl seemed to like it too, but "One" thought it was a disgusting show of sex. It seemed to me that "One" was becoming a prude.

Looking down from Daryl's lap, I noticed a beautiful male Dachshund next to Mother. I squirmed out of Daryl's lap to get down to meet the fellow. "One" and "Three" were already getting acquainted with him, and I didn't want to be left out. (By the way, not wanting to be left out of anything is a Dachshund trait.) As I approached Mother and my two sisters, I wondered if this might be the father, that mystery fellow that Mother kept in the dark from us all this time. And surely enough, that is exactly who this good-looking "Hot Dog" of a guy was.

My sisters and I were disappointed in the reception we received from our father. He tolerated us, but that was about it. Mother told us that he was interested in just one thing: SEX!!!! He did lead a very interesting life and got to travel a lot. He even got to travel by air, and was always treated like royalty. Mother had told us that he was a real champion, an "international champion"; a mouthful especially for my small mouth.

Daryl, who seemed to be in charge of everything, had reduced that mighty mouthful to simply, "Oscar." (I could handle that.) My sisters and I finally realized that the reason for his inattention to us, was that he was impressed with himself. He was a very important "dude." And why not, since he had fathered many, many other Dachshund families all over the world, not to mention the dozen or so right here in the kennel and right under Mother's nose. He was always very much in demand for the job. He was a part of Daryl's highly respected staff, and Daryl advertised him in specialty magazines and professional papers as being "at stud," whatever that means. It sounded like a good job, though, with all the travel and adoration that this fellow got, and with no responsibility whatsoever after committing the deed. I told Mother later that that is exactly what I wanted to be when I grew up. She just smiled a weary little smile and said, "I don't think so, Dear."

Our father hung around for a short while, paying no attention to us. But he did spend some time doing quite a lot of intensive sniffing and pawing around Mother. It pleased us to see Mother give him the cold look and practically ignore his advances. However this guy knew what he was looking for, and was not to be discouraged. Soon Daryl introduced him to a complete stranger who looked a lot like Mother. He dropped Mother at once and started some intensive sniffing and rapid tail wagging. Daryl led the two of them away. Mother explained to us that Oscar was about to start another family. She didn't seem to mind at all. I felt really bad seeing the two of them being led away, both wagging their tails and oozing happiness. This is the last time I ever saw him, but all things considered it is probably better to have the sex-hound out of our lives . . . the rogue!!!

Growing Up

The next few weeks we were allowed a lot of freedom. Daryl took us away from Mother and started feeding us really yummy food which he called "science diet." It was a lot different than the food Mother had provided and which we had enjoyed so much in our earlier days. This stuff had real body to it. Of course, the stuff Mother had provided had body too (her body). Daryl didn't allow us to pee on his green lawn, because it made brown spots, so he started training us to go over to the side yard. It seemed as though life was becoming very complicated with rules, rules, rules and more rules. Things were changing very fast for the three of us. We still saw Mother every day, but her attention toward us seemed to be waning.

I decided to be just a little bit naughty, and now and then, when no one was watching, I would do a little pee on Daryl's lawn anyway, just to add a little interest to my life, and to convince myself that I was still in charge. I knew that the spot wouldn't turn brown for a few days, and even though Daryl might be angry, he'd have no way of knowing who did it. And even if he did suspect me, I'd just try to look cute, wag my tail, and in extreme cases, give him one of my slurpy kisses. That would nearly always get me off the hook with Daryl, no matter what manner of mischief I'd been up to.

Most of our days were becoming routine: eating, playing with my two sisters, sleeping (we took lots of naps), and just exploring the area. I was more curious and active than "One" and "Three" when it came to exploring. I discovered that Mother and the three of us were not alone. The place we lived in was called a kennel and there were many other canines (all Dachshunds) in different areas living there raising small families. Some were all tan, and many were black and tan like my mother and the three of us triplets. Some even had long hair.

Although there were many Dachshunds in the kennel, I realized that Daryl liked me best when one day he picked me up and took me into his house. Wow, did I ever explore then! There were interesting smells I had never smelled before, under beds and in closets. The smells under Daryl's bed were so wonderful that I crawled under the bed and went to sleep. Daryl looked everywhere for me, and when he finally found me he seemed a little angry. Remembering Mother's teachings, I just licked his hand, and when he picked me up I gave him one of my now famous slurpies. This brought about instant forgiveness, as usual. Then Daryl carried me into his study, and wow, did I ever learn a lot in there. The walls were lined with blue ribbons. As Mother had indicated, all of my relatives were champions. Looking at all of those blue ribbons, I realized what she meant when she had said we were all "blue bloods." Up until then that term had made no sense, because I knew that my blood was red.

At the time we had been born, the kennel was full, so Daryl had put Mother in the main house in a closet-type room next to his study. This made us feel rather superior to those others who lived out in the kennel. Daryl spent a lot of time in his study listening to television, and at last I realized what the noises were that came through the door into our little cubicle. That door opened directly into the small room where the three of us were born and where

Mother had raised us. When Daryl opened that door and put me back in our room, I really felt empowered, and started walking around with my nose in the air. I soon realized, however, that since my nose is extra long, it is difficult to act snooty and hold it in the air for long periods of time. As a matter of fact, as I have grown older, I am always more comfortable if I can rest that long nose on someone's arm, on the arm of a chair, or on anything else that happens to be available. I think that perhaps when I get older and can find the right doctor, I might consider a "nose job." But, I suppose the inconvenience of "longnoseiness" is offset by the fantastic smells I can get with it.

"One"

"One" was one strange puppy from the beginning, and of late she had become even a bit snobbish and stuffy. Because she was the oldest of the three, she seemed to try to boss me and "Three," and she let it be known that she didn't approve of many of my antics. Even when Mother had told us that we were dogs, "One" was not bothered by the idea at all, but seemed to relish the idea that we were somehow the back side of God, which made us special. I later knew how she knew so much about God. Mother told us as a puppy, "One" would slip out of bed at night and put her ear against the door that led into Daryl's study.

Daryl was a religious fellow and often listened to television far into the night. He was especially interested in a program called *Mysteries of the Bible.* He also has a lot of tapes dealing with the Bible which interested him. "One" developed a keen interest in what she heard, and one day told us of a reading called the Lord's Prayer which she had memorized. She said it to herself several times every day. It didn't make much sense to me except the part about "Give us this day our daily bread." I liked that part even though I'm not particularly fond of bread. Chicken and that science diet are just fine with me. She also said that if someone does something bad to you and you forgive them, then it's OK to do the same thing to them or to someone else. I've made that saying a part of my life. For example, I got entangled with a cat once, and the wretch scratched me. I forgave the cat, so now I figure it's OK to chase any cat I can find, and forgiveness will follow. And I really do love to chase cats any time I can find one. Now and then, one will stand his ground and turn on me. When that happens, I turn tail and run as fast as I can, screaming and forgiving him as I run. The cat never chases me, so I guess that's the way that Lord's Prayer thing works. Anyway, it works for me.

But, to get back to my weird sister, "One." Even though Mother had become more disinterested in us, she called us together one day to let us know we were going to be split up. We were all going to different places where we would have servants to care for us. We'd have chauffeurs, nice homes, and others to care for us, and it was going to happen soon. The next day, two Catholic nuns came to the kennel to take "One" away with them. It was sad to see her go, but she was overjoyed. She would be able to continue her learning about God. She would be living in a convent with many nuns as her servants, and she would have a new name. From now on she would be known as "Sister Robert." That seemed an odd name for a Dachshund, but probably more interesting than the one Mother had given her at birth. Besides, she could be the first Dachshund nun in the history of the Church. As she was leaving, she confided in me that she hoped she could be cute enough to win the heart of the Mother Superior and eventually get to sleep on her bed.

"Three" and New York

In a few days I learned that "Three" would be leaving us for a new home in upstate New York. This meant that she would be flying in an airplane to a new life. I was jealous and felt left out. I started worrying that I would be left in the kennel and end up with a job like Mother's; that is, until I learned the whole story. Daryl had advertised in a classy specialty magazine, with a picture of "Three" as being for sale. A kennel in New York, recognizing her championship blood, jumped at the chance to add our bloodline to theirs. This meant, of course, that "Three" would be in the breeding business!!! She would have litter after litter of babies until she became too old and tired to carry on. I shuddered at the thought, and was so grateful that it was, "Three" and not me. I couldn't imagine a job like that with litter after litter, and suck, suck, suck, lick, lick, lick, wipe, wipe wipe and push, push, push!!! And just when you get over the last bunch, someone like our father appears, gleefully does his thing and then leaves, and the whole process starts over again. Yikes!! That's enough to make a girl hide under the bed and never come out.

Well, I was one lonely puppy for the next several days. With "One" and "Three" both gone, life didn't seem much fun. And Mother was certainly no fun; she was expecting another family and we had very little time together. She soon called me aside however and told me that shortly after the three of us were born, a nice fellow from Carmel, California, a small village by the sea, had visited the kennel. After a long conversation with Daryl, he had chosen me as "Pick of the Litter" to be with him when I was old enough to leave home. Yikes, that probably saved me from having to live my life in a convent like "One" or from being shipped off to New York to a life of domestic drudgery like "Three." Mother didn't know much about this fellow except that his name was Jim, and he had arrived in a little red convertible the day he chose me. Yikes, things were beginning to look great for my future. Jim would arrive tomorrow. I could hardly wait.

Life with Daddy Jim

To tell the truth, I was a nervous wreck! I slept hardly at all that night, for I kept imagining what Jim would be like and what it would be like to be with him. Would I have a new name, and if so, would it be a name I liked? Would my new home have a place for me to run and play? Would I be allowed to pee on the lawn (my favorite place)? I had so many questions running through my little Dachshund brain that I was almost giddy. But, early in the morning my waiting came to an end. Jim arrived just as Mother had said he would in OUR little red convertible. It was really a cool car, and to think that it was now MINE made me really happy.

When Jim picked me up and held me close to his face, I gave him one of my best slurpies right across the mouth. That may have seemed a little bold to be so outgoing on what might be called our "first date," but I wanted this fellow to know right from the beginning that I did not intend to be just some little subservient thing with no ideas of my own. Actually, I wanted him to realize that I planned to be in charge of things! As matter of fact, I liked Jim from the first moment I saw him, and he seemed to be very pleased with me and my kisses. He was truly a handsome fellow, sun-tanned, I suspected from riding with the top down in that convertible.

Jim had brought along a little cage, and inside was the softest blanket I had ever seen. He held me and petted me, petted my mother and talked with Daryl. The matter of a name for me came up, and I held my breath while they were deciding. When I heard it I almost fainted. My name was to be "Sandar's Isabella Brown Dukey." I didn't like it at all. I had a name, but it is no better than "Two," the name Mother gave me. Yipes, "Isabella" for a German "Blue Blood"!!!

Makes no sense at all. I do wish that these people who continue to think they are in charge, would either show some intelligence in choosing names for us, or let us name ourselves. I had hoped for something like "Gretchen" or "Schatze," but "Isabella"!!! Well, I think I'll just keep my maiden name of "Two" and let it go at that. Let them call me what they will. They'll never know the difference.

The ride in our little convertible was wild. I was so thrilled, but also half scared most of the time. I'd never done this before, and it is the things we know little about that hold the greatest fear, I think. I hated that little cage, and whined to get out, and finally, Jim stopped the car and let me out to sit in the passenger seat. Then, as we sped along, I put my nose over the side, let my ears blow in the wind, and I took in all the great smells of the countryside. The important thing here was that just a few little whines got me what I wanted (out of that cage). Daddy Jim was probably going to be easy to train.

When we arrived in Carmel at my new home, I could hardly believe it. I had a wonderful backyard to run and play in. There were many plants, a great lawn, and the smell of pine trees and the nearby ocean were almost intoxicating. I knew I was going to love my new life, and I also knew that I needed to start bonding with Daddy Jim as soon as possible. This didn't take long, and I knew that I was already worming my way into his heart with just acting cute and sticking close to him. Our little beach house was well furnished with lots of Oriental stuff, and Oriental rugs that Daddy Jim had brought back from China on one of his many trips there.

One evening after a long day, we settled into a big comfy chair for a nap. Jim was tired and dozed off, and because I wasn't tired at all, I decided that this would be a good time to do more exploring around my new digs. After sniffling around a bit, I decided to try out the Orientals. I had a feeling they would be even better than a grassy lawn. I was in the middle of a prolonged pee when Daddy Jim awakened and caught me in the act. Needless to say, all the so-called bonding of that day went up in blue smoke. We came un-bonded in a hurry.

Daddy Jim tossed me outside and made it very clear that I was never again to "weedle" in the house. I had never heard it called that before, and it was beginning to look as though I might be learning a whole new language. Weedle, indeed!!! Jim made me stay outside for a long time, so I crawled under the porch and tried to think of some cute thing I could do to restore our bonding. So when he finally opened the door. I slunk in with my tail between my legs and dredged up the saddest look I could think of on my little black and tan face. And, by yippers, it worked. He felt sorry for me. He picked me up and held me close. I wagged my tail, started to smile and gave him a slurp across the mouth. All was forgiven!

Mother was right; cuteness, if played right, can get a girl almost anything she wants, especially, out of trouble.

Of course, every day was not rosy for me. I just couldn't resist that Oriental rug, and I went on it several more times, each time getting into trouble and having to wriggle my way out. I also had to learn a new word, "doodle." Mother had another word for it too, which I'll not mention in print. Anyway, I learned about "weedle" and "doodle" and realized finally that Daddy Jim didn't like such things on the Orientals. This was finally solved when I got it across to Jim that when I barked at the door it was a sign that I needed to go outside to do one or the other. Maybe both!!

Wonderful days passed. Jim took me to the beach almost daily and let me run free. There were many other canines there (notice that I prefer "canines" to "dogs" since it sounds more sophisticated), along with their people companions playing on the beach. Daddy Jim and I made friends with them very easily. And I got to know a lot of them in short order. There were no cats to chase. I did have fun, though, chasing after seagulls. They would always run from me, and just as I was within biting range, they would take to the air and fly away. Perhaps one day I can take flying lessons, and then I'd be able to catch one.

Jim and I kept bonding. He took me to his office to meet all of his friends and employees. Right away they started buying treats for me which they kept in their desk drawers. I learned quickly where the best treats were kept, so I always worked the crowd, and hit the best drawers first.

At home we became the best of pals, and the bonding became stronger day by day. We even had an occasional bath together, and I finally trained Jim to let me sleep with him. What a life!!! I often wondered if my big sister, "Sister Robert," was sleeping with the Mother Superior. I would bet on it.

I learned that Daddy Jim's work required him to travel a lot, and on one of his trips he took me with him to New York. This was very exciting for me since it involved traveling by air. I thought to myself that my roguish father and "brood sow" sister have nothing on me. Daddy

Jim and I were actually flying first class, and while I was allowed aboard in my little cage that was stowed under the seat in front of Jim, once we were airborne, he let me out and held me on his lap. I was an instant hit with the stewardesses and the other passengers around us, and first class food is really great. Even though Jim had me on that science diet stuff most of the time, he gave me a nibble of his fillet mignon, and when the stewardess saw how much I liked it, she brought me one of my own. I really reveled in this trip since I was pretty sure that my father and my sister "Three" had probably had to go "cargo," and here I was, going first class.

After the New York trip, Jim announced that his business required him to travel to China, and since the New York trip had been such a success, he was planning to take me along. Well, take me along indeed!!! Mother had warned us in one of our training sessions to stay out of China at all costs since they eat our kind over there just as we do chickens and cows over here in this country. The very thought of going to China scared the "weedle" out of me. I was so upset by the thought that I hid under the bed and whined for two days. I pretended to be sick and put on a long, sad face. Finally someone told Jim that if he didn't keep a sharp look out I might end up on a dinner plate with noodles. That made my blood run cold. Daddy Jim just laughed and said, "She wouldn't make a good hors d'oeuvre." Anyway, it didn't work out because there wasn't time for him to get the necessary shots and papers together before the trip. Thank God for that. I felt so relieved! When he realized that he was not going to be able to take me along, Daddy Jim said, "I guess it's about time for you to meet some of my family anyway, and since I'll be gone for about ten days you'll need a nice place to stay." That's when I met Auntie "O."

Auntie "O"

Olivia is Daddy Jim's sister. She lives in a neat little beach house about a hundred miles south of Carmel. Jim took me down in our convertible to spend a few days while he was away. I knew I would miss Jim a lot, but this was better than being left in a kennel with a bunch of dogs, and certainly better than being a morsel on someone's chopstick at a banquet in China. Besides, I was about to experience ten days with a real character.

She referred to herself as my Auntie "O," and no sooner had Jim driven away than she poured me a saucer of milk. I must have given her a dumb look because I was shocked!! Did she think I was a cat??? When she realized that I wouldn't lap milk, she prepared me a dish of chopped Caribou meat. I had never tasted Caribou before. It had a bit of a wild taste to it which was really not bad, and was really a lot better than acting like a cat and learning to lap milk. Jim had brought along enough canned science diet to last me for the ten-day stay, but Auntie "O" didn't own a can opener, and didn't eat anything from cans herself. We went for long walks on the beach, where I had my usual failures at chasing sea gulls. We bonded very quickly, and she loved my sloppy kisses across her lips. She wanted to hold me on her lap while she watched television, but I wriggled down because I found it just too boring to sit there and do nothing. One time when I wriggled down I chewed up one of her new

21

shoes, and another time I chewed some holes in a pair of her panties which she had carelessly left on the floor. I like to keep busy doing things.

There was a small creamery in town, and on one of our walks, we stopped by and Auntie "O" bought us an ice cream cone. She would take a bite and then give me a lick. I was sure that Daddy Jim would not approve of this diet, but I ate it anyway, partly to be polite, but mostly because it was so good, even though it did give me diarrhea. Auntie "O" and I were really bonding, and I didn't have to beg to get into her bed that night. It was her idea, and while we snuggled in for a cozy night together I wondered about "Sister Robert." Was she in bed with the Mother Superior?

The next morning we had a breakfast of more Caribou. Auntie "O" is able to get the stuff from a very good friend in Alaska who lives a little north of the Arctic Circle. His name is Schrimsha, and he goes into the wilds up there, hunts the Caribou, and then sends Auntie "O" a hunk of frozen meat. Frankly, I prefer the science diet stuff that Jim feeds me. That afternoon she thought it would be fun to paint my nails, and before I knew it, I was parading around with red painted nails, both front and rear! I thought for awhile it made me look a bit like a hussy, but in a little while, I realized that I was cuter than ever. I wished that I could go back to Daryl's kennel and show my mother my new cuteness. However, I shudder to think what my big nun sister, Sister Robert, would think of me. She was always so proper. After my nails were really dry, Auntie "O" wanted to show me off, so we made another trip to the ice cream parlor, and more ice cream which we shared lick by lick even though I had learned what it did to my poor little tummy. But it was so good. This time chocolate!

The next day, Auntie "O" bought me a new collar made with big stainless steel studs. It's the type they put on rotweilers or pit bulls, but she had it made in my size. It seemed really too heavy for me to carry around, especially with my long nose already trying to overbalance me. However, as Mother had taught us, I acted grateful, and pleased with the gift and the attention that Auntie "O" was showering upon me.

I was probably acting a bit too grateful for my own good, because once she saw how pleased I seemed to be with my "new look," she brought forth a good-sized diamond earring from her jewelery box. Before I cold say "yipes" she had pierced my right ear, and had me wearing a diamond earring. I believe she thought that it made me look cuter, and I felt that I was really living at the top of society. And we both enjoyed the admiring looks we got from folks when we took walks downtown with my red toenails, steel studded collar, and diamond earring. It was an exciting time for both of us. Anyway, I didn't get to wear the earring when I went home. It was to be our little secret, and Auntie "O" took it off just two days before Jim came to take me home. I was just beginning to get used to it, and I knew that I would miss the admiring looks I enjoyed so much. Auntie "O" would keep the diamond until I came to visit again.

Daddy Jim returned just in the nick of time, because Auntie "O" was planning to do something to my tail. I was fearful that she might be planning to install a tail light, or perhaps curl it. I never learned what the actual plan was, but it scared me to think of the possibilities. Jim never learned about the earring, and the polish finally wore off my nails. It was good to get off the Caribou chow and back to Daddy Jim and the science diet. I knew I'd be seeing Auntie "O" again, and I do miss her. I regret that there wasn't enough time on my first visit to give her the training she needs. She did learn, however, not to leave her shoes and panties on the floor when I am visiting.

When I got home to Carmel, life became even more exciting. I met Willie.

Willie

The first thing we noticed when we got back to our little cottage in Carmel, was that during the time we had been away some new neighbors had moved into the vacant house next door. They were a fun-filled couple named Patricia and Alex Lang, and they had a wonderful young puppy. He was part Affenpinscher and had several breeds mixed in. At least he was part German with that Affenpinscher blood. I believe he was also part Chihuahua. Like me, he had his own backyard for romping and playing and for doing all of those other things that we are required to do in the backyard rather than in the house. He had one of those long names that people like to give to their canine friends. Because of his mostly German blood, the Langs had named him, "Kaiser Wilhelm Something, that seemed to go on forever," and was much too difficult for me to remember or even to say. But, Pat and Alex called him Willie for short which made it easier for me.

Willie was, perhaps, the ugliest little fellow I had ever seen. He had short grey hair that was a bit kinky in places, and little tufts of hair around his feet. He had long spindly legs for his size and was a little taller than I am. That doesn't mean he's tall though, since I'm only a couple inches from the ground myself. And he had a face like a wizened old man and whiskers a bit like a cat. He was so ugly that he was one of the cutest pups I had ever seen. And he bubbled with personality. We became friends at once, and saw each other often since Daddy Jim and the Langs liked to take us for walks in the evening together. They also often took us to the beach and let us romp together on nice days.

One time when Pat asked Daddy Jim if he could look after Willie when they had to be away for a few days, I was overjoyed when it was decided that Willie would stay with us. They brought over Willie's special food and his dish and his bed. I was glad about the dish because I don't like for anyone to eat out of my dish. That is one thing I didn't want to share with him even though we had become steadfast pals. It's just too personal!! I did think it would be nice to sleep together, but Jim put us in our own beds. However, once Jim went to sleep, I crept out of my bed and spent the night curled up next to Willie.

It was Heaven, but Daddy Jim didn't think much of the idea when he found us together the next morning. After that first night he put my little bed in the bathroom with the door shut, and Willie slept in the kitchen. That matter seemed a little Victorian on Jim's part, and besides, I felt sorry for poor Willie having to sleep alone. I also felt that he might think that I was not being a very good hostess. Jim said that I shouldn't get too serious with Willie, and that even though he was mostly Affenpinscher he was till not my type since he was a mutt, whatever that means!! I think most dads are that way about their girls.

After the Langs returned home, and came over for Willie, I didn't see much of him, since Jim kept an eye on me and kept me at home. He seemed a bit suspicious of what we might be doing. Willie and I would yipe at each other now and then through our fence, and that was our only contact for several weeks. Well, one day we became so lonely to see each other that we decided to dig ourselves a tunnel under the fence. I dug from my side and Willie dug from his side. My digging was under a large hydrangea bush and Jim didn't see my digging. Willie had a large overgrown vine over his hole. Once finished, we could slip through our little secret tunnel and play to our hearts' content.

Jim often left me in my yard for the entire day when the weather was good and he was at his office. So on those days I saw a lot of Willie. Both Pat and Alex worked, and they left Willie outside too, so no one knew of our little secret. We would spend hours chasing each other around both backyards, and finally when we grew tired we would curl up in a warm sunny spot and have a nap together.

I noticed one day that Willie was beginning to change his attitude toward me a little bit. He seemed to be losing his "puppyness" and displaying more of his "maleness." I was changing too, in my feelings for Willie. I was beginning to think of him as more than just a friend that I could romp and play with, and more like a friend that I wanted to be with all of the time. Then it hit me. Willie and I were falling in love!!

He spent a lot of time sniffing around me, just like my roguish father used to do with Mother and other bitches at Daryl's place. And it bothered me that I liked it. I liked his sniffing and his attention. He seemed to adore me, and we always hated it when Jim or the Langs got home and we had to make hasty retreats through the tunnel to our own yards.

We actually considered digging a new tunnel under one of our fences and running away, but one day while we were digging, Daddy Jim came home and caught us red-handed. I was in Willie's yard and we were both digging. Jim discovered my tunnel under the hydrangea bush and promptly filled it up with small rocks. He took me into our house and again said that Willie was not my type and that I should have nothing more to do with him. Furthermore, the next day he took me to the Vet (whom I hated) to have my teeth cleaned, and while I was knocked out the wretch performed a little surgery on me and removed my "puppy machine." He robbed me of my "bitch-hood"!!! I was furious with all of them, and especially with Daddy Jim for letting it happen.

After I recovered, I did see Willie occasionally but he had lost most of his interest in me, and I no longer wanted to dig myself out of my yard and run away with him. Also, I finally got over my anger with Daddy Jim, but I still hate the Vet.

I love to sleep on Jim's bed.

Me and "our" red convertible.

Could I be any cuter?

After my first bath.

A weedle on an oriental rug was great until
Daddy Jim caught me.

Beds are some of my favorite places.

After my bath, I get to dry out on a big thick towel and lie in the sun.

Of course, sofas are pretty nice places, too!

I finally got my way concerning Dogma and her car.

Doing community service with "3d Paw."

Me and a new friend on Carmel Beach.

Canines are allowed to run free on Carmel Beach, and I've made many friends there.

Daddy Jim and me.

"3d Paw" and "Dogma"

I had a very hard time getting over my love affair with Willie, and Daddy Jim seemed to take on an even more protective attitude toward me. Rather than leave me alone in the backyard, he decided to take me to his parents' home to spend the day when he was in his office. They had just returned to Carmel after several months of travel, and he thought that it would be better for me to be with them than alone in my backyard with Willie on the other side of my fence.

They had a large home not too far from where Jim and I lived. Jim explained that I would be their "grand dog," and that they would be my "dog paw" and "dog maw." I was really interested in meeting them, but it gave me the willies that I couldn't get it across to Jim that the word "dog" when referring to me frustrated me. I consider myself to be a Dachshund, not a dog! Why not use the words "Dachshund Paw" and "Dachshund Ma"? Or really, why not spell it backwards and call it "Grand God," "God Paw," and "God Maw"? That's the way my sister "One" explained it when we were younger.

I have always maintained that I am NOT a dog and especially since I once saw a real dog walking along the highway with his keeper. They appeared to be homeless. The poor thing looked half-starved, dirty and flea-ridden. And even though he seemed to love his keeper as much as

I love my Daddy Jim, I won't be one of those, ever. But it all worked out for me, as most things do.

They have a house with a stairway which I found at once, and enjoyed running up and down. What a life! They knew we were coming, so they had some treats for me and a nice new blue dish which was bigger and better than the one I have at our house. (Eating utensils are very important to Dachshunds.) I just could not think of Jim's father as "Dog Paw," and since I already have four paws of my own I decided to think of him as "third paw," or "3d Paw," or simply "3d 🐾." Now, finding a suitable handle for Jim's mother was a different matter. She didn't like to be referred to as "Maw" by anyone. She even had her own grandchildren call her "Dearest." She was always very proper and, like me, she was of German descent. And like me, she could sometimes be very stubborn. After a lot of thought, I decided that I'd think of her as "Dogma." That just seemed to fit her perfectly, and with an entirely different meaning than if it were separated in the middle. I could live with that!

So, it did work out for me, "3d 🐾" and "Dogma." I was destined to spend many happy hours with them with long walks on the beach, along the river, and through Mission Park along the many trails. I was beginning to realize that instead of having one nice home as Mother had promised that I now had at least three.

I worried a lot about all of these new people coming into my life, since I didn't speak their language and they didn't speak mine. And considering the difficulty I was still having in training Daddy Jim, I knew that there was still a lot of training left for me to do. "3d 🐾" and I, from the beginning always got along great. To a degree, he and I did speak the same language: body language. I learned that I could just look at him and he had a way of under-standing what I wanted or needed.

If I happened to be thirsty and my water dish was low, a certain look would always bring water. Once I learned to tell time, I knew exactly when four-thirty in the afternoon came around, and a certain look would let him know that it was time for him to start getting my dinner ready. If he happened to be taking a nap in his reclining chair, a soft little whine on my part followed with a gentle scratch on the side of the chair meant that I would like to join him, and he would always pick me up and let me cozy in beside him.

"3d 🐾" and I had very little trouble communicating, except when he wanted me to do something that I didn't want to do. At times like that I would simply walk away, or walk into another room in the house and lie down. That way, he couldn't read my body language or look into my eyes so our lines of communication were severed. "3d 🐾" drove a big car, and sometimes would take me with him.

At first, I didn't like it since I was used to riding in our little red convertible with the top down. However, I soon trained "3d 🐾" to let me sit on his lap and help him drive. He learned quickly that I like having my nose out the window while we drive. There is not much in a Dachshund's life that is more fun than speeding along the highway with ears flopping and our noses sucking in the great smells as we watch the scenery change. What a riot. "3d 🐾" was fairly easy to train, and seemed to enjoy being able to figure out what I wanted to do.

One of my greatest training successes, however, was with Daddy Jim, when he tried to train me (of all things) to fetch a ball. Everyone should know that Dachshunds don't fetch. This was a hard training lesson for Jim, and I finally changed the rules a bit to keep him from taking it so hard. He would throw the ball and I would run to get it, but instead of returning it to him as he wanted, I would run in the opposite direction. He finally understood my revised rules of fetching, and realized that he was supposed to catch me and retrieve the ball himself. It is a much more civilized game, and one designed to give Daddy Jim some of the exercise he needs. And besides, I have fun doing it with him.

The other so-called "tricks" that Jim or anyone else tried to get me to do all ended in failure on their part. I don't roll over. I don't play dead. (There will be lots of time for that down the line.) I don't shake hands or paws with anyone; I don't heel; I don't sit up; I don't speak; I don't do any of those silly things which are probably OK for poodles or boxers, but for me, No way!!

However, I did get into serious trouble once, by chasing a ball that belonged to one of my countrymen, a German Shepherd. One time while staying with Dogma and "3d ❧" I noticed a neighbor who every evening exercised his German Shepherd by throwing a yellow tennis ball down the street in front of our house. The German Shepherd was named Queenie, and as she ran by our yard on her way to retrieve the ball, she paid me no attention even though I always barked hysterically as she lunged by to capture the ball and return it to her owner.

He was a handsome Marine Corps captain, and he had her well-trained. She knew that she was to ignore my barking and to concentrate on fetching that ball. Day after day I fumed over this situation until one day I could stand it no longer.

As I saw the ball approaching, I squirmed under our gate, ran into the street and grabbed the ball, with the idea of wriggling back under the gate and making the ball my very own, and in the meantime letting Queenie rage outside the fence, because she was too big to squirm under the gate. Well, it didn't work that way at all. Sooner than expected, Queenie was upon me. She mouthed me and rolled me around. I was covered with saliva and dust from the street.

Fearing that I was about to become her evening meal, I screamed as loudly as I could. My screaming called out the Marine Captain and Daddy Jim. I had not one mark on me, but I was filthy dirty and a nervous wreck. The Marine officer and Jim became good friends. Queenie continued to fetch the ball every evening, and I simply sat there by the gate as the ball and Queenie went by.

I was fuming within but out of better judgment I held my bark down to a low inward growl. I then remembered something that my big sister had once said when she was talking about God, something about do not covet, but it wasn't specific about yellow tennis balls. And Queenie, I believe, never realized that I was really trying to help her. I wanted to get that ball and hide it so that she'd never again have to fetch again. The poor thing.

Since everything always works out for me in the long run, I ended up with my own tennis ball in just a few days. "3d 🐾" and I went for a walk a few days after the Queenie incident, and while walking by a tennis club, I spotted my own yellow tennis ball. "3d 🐾" felt that it wasn't mine and that I should leave it where I found it or turn it in at the club house. I knew doggoned well that it was mine since I found it, and since I held onto it with all my jaw strength, "3d 🐾" allowed me to keep it. After all, I wasn't stealing it or coveting it so it was mine.

We were quite some distance from home, and I was determined to hang onto my new find until I got back to my own yard. Well, with my long nose, short legs, and heavy tennis ball, I soon became tired and put down the ball. This is where my early training of "3d 🐾" paid off. After giving him my look of "please help me," he knew exactly what I needed, and he picked up the ball and carried it for me the rest of the way home. Once at home, however, there was never any question about who owned the ball. I OWNED IT!!! I FOUND IT, AND IT WAS MINE.

However, Dogma didn't always see things my way, so she started to take my ball away from me and put it outside. Since she had been exceedingly difficult to train, I decided to use unusual measures to let her know that the ball belonged to me. I found it, and it was mine. I knew I shouldn't do it, but I did it anyway for the sake of her training. I growled a low warning growl, and then I snapped at her. I didn't touch her, I simply snapped, and whack! whack! whack! She slapped my rear, and I yiped to high heaven. Then she pushed me outside and tossed the ball out after me. There was no doubt about who was in charge.

I spent the afternoon in the yard sulking in a nice sunny spot on the patio. When Jim came to pick me up and found that I had been banished to the outside for the afternoon, he asked "3d 🐾" who had banished me, and he replied, "You know who." I thought that Unohoo was a strange name for anyone, especially for Dogma.

Dogma and I had a hard time getting along because it seemed that I was always doing something that displeased her. As an example, she didn't like for me to bark. With me, barking just comes naturally, and most of the time, I can't help it. It's like wagging my tail. I can't help that either. One evening Dogma had the hiccups and couldn't stop. "3d 🐾" pointed out that perhaps my barking was like her hiccups and I couldn't stop even if I wanted to. (And sometimes, I honestly didn't want to stop.) Anyway this seemed to make her a little kinder toward me, even though he told Daddy Jim that sometimes my barking drove her "nuts." I was grateful that "3d 🐾" had taken on the job of helping me train Dogma.

On many occasions when Dogma was fed up with my barking, she would put me outside and shut the sliding glass door. On one warm day, only the sliding screen door was closed, and having been banished to the outside for a longer period than I thought necessary, I simply clawed a Dachshund-sized hole through the screen and came on in anyway. Of course, Dogma was furious with me, but she didn't learn a thing with this training episode.

A week later, I was exiled to the outside again, and another screen for a sliding glass door was left unattended. I ripped out my second hole and came inside, because I wanted to. And this time the training worked! Dogma finally learned that banishment did very little good, and from then on she left the door open just enough so that I could come and go as I pleased.

This was a small victory for me, but very hard-won. I believe that without the help of "3d 🐾" she would never have learned! Later, one of our neighbors referred to me as "The neighborhood nine-pound terror" since I barked so much and chased cats and birds. Dogma replied, "not the 'neighborhood terror.' The 'screen tearer' is a far better description." This was the first I realized that Dogma had a sense of humor. I was making progress.

I had rather quickly convinced Daddy Jim to let me sit on his lap while he drove our convertible. While I had never had any formal driver training, I caught on in a hurry, and Jim always let me sit on his lap and help. I never watched the road since that was his job; my job was to hang my nose out the window and smell stuff. "3d 🐾" let me sit on his lap, too and let me help drive. He always let me have the window down. I could sit on his lap, hang my head out the window and give my nose a great work-out.

I have always looked at cars as scenery changing ma-chines. Of course, getting to have my head out the window when Dogma was driving was an entirely different mat-ter. Not only would she not let me sit on her lap and help drive with my nose out the window, she made me sit in the passenger seat with the window rolled up. She didn't like her hair to blow in the wind. I found the whole thing a bit stuffy, especially for my nose.

Dogma liked a clean car always, and often when we went to the car wash she should take me along. I liked that. She would always put me on a leash to keep me out of trouble while her car was being washed. The car always came out jewel-like with crystal-clear windows. Dogma was always very pleased and said that her car seemed to run better when it was clean.

Well, on one car wash day, I had a stupendous idea. When unleashed and placed in the passenger seat, I stood on my hind legs and rubbed my nose all over the clean window. I licked it too. Dogma was busy driving and did-n't notice what I was doing until we got home. When she noticed the window it was a real mess, and although I knew that she would be furious with me, I figured that this training session was necessary since it was either her hair or my nose! And my nose won out, because from that day forward, she left the windows down for me and she wore a scarf to keep her hair from blowing. Really, we both won a little on that one since she looks really beauti-ful with her hair in a scarf. She still won't let me help her drive, but I'm still working on it.

Auntie Anne and Tucker

About the time I thought I'd seen everything, Daddy Jim and I stopped by a very beautiful apartment one evening, and I was introduced to Auntie Anne. Auntie Anne had just returned from a world trip, and she had refurnished her apartment with antiques which she had purchased in Spain. Everything was really lavish. Auntie Anne was very rich and Daddy Jim said that most of her wealth came from her job. Seems she married for a living! She had divorced several husbands and two or three had died rather mysteriously, and all left her better off financially than she had been with the previous one. Jim said it was far better than compound interest or the stock market.

Auntie Anne was very pretty and took very good care of herself. She had to; her job required it. Anyway, among all the lavishness was a large iron cage, and perched atop the cage was a parrot she had somehow smuggled in from the Amazon. His name was Tucker. While Tucker lived in the cage, most of the time he was allowed to sit on top and squawk, or yell or scream. Actually, he could sing a little opera which Auntie Anne had taught him. He was a real noise-maker, and I was really glad that he didn't belong to Daddy Jim and me.

From moment one, I thought that if I could catch him, it would make up for all the gulls that had escaped on the wing when I chased them on the beach. He seemed to give me a sort of evil eye, so I think he was as curious about me as I was about him. I presumed that if I got a chance to chase him that he would take flight just like all the others. He probably thought that I was the first intelligent being he'd seen in some time, since he spent his life in and on top of that cage, notwithstanding that it was a Spanish antique.

Tucker became so curious about me that he made a leap from his cage and landed on the floor almost under my nose. I realized that his wings were clipped and that he couldn't fly.

Joy, oh joy, I thought! Here was my chance to get one of those feathered critters into my little belly and to find out at last if it was worth my time to chase them anyway. I made a short leap, grabbed that bird, and started carrying him into the next room where I intended to have an early dinner.

Tucker let out a blood-curdling scream! Auntie Anne and Daddy Jim in the next room heard the commotion and came running. I had Tucker in my mouth and was beginning to shake him, when Auntie Anne made a flying leap through the air, grabbed my throat and made me drop my prey.

Poor Tucker was a total wreck, and even though he did recover, I suspect that he is still having nightmares about our encounter. As for me, I was disappointed that having finally caught one of those critters I had to let it go. I just sat there with a green tail feather in my mouth looking sad and probably a little stupid while Auntie Anne and Jim gave me a tongue lashing. I never have felt that this little incident was really my fault, even though from that day until now I have been "Doggona nongrata" at Auntie Anne's place.

Dachshund Math

I have always been interested in many things such as eating, sleeping, chasing cats and birds, training others, and helping folks drive cars. But I never intended to study math until one day Jim took me to the Vet's for a "booster" shot (which I also dislike). I heard them talking about the facts of life (My Life). Never had I realized that there was an end to all this, and that my life would end seven times faster than Daddy Jim's. In other words, if Jim lives for one year, then whoosh, I've gone through seven years. Wow!

In other words, if Daddy Jim were in my shoes, so to speak, he'd be, well, dead! Well, I already hated the Vet for the things he had done to me such as shots on a routine basis, plus the hysterectomy he did against my will which destroyed my bitchhood at an early age. Now my dislike for him was greater than ever because he gave me something to worry about that would never have crossed my mind. One hour equals seven hours! One day equals seven days! One week equals seven weeks! Yikes! One month equals seven months! Why shouldn't we get to eat fourteen times a day? Why shouldn't Dachshund Christmas come seven times a year? These were things that I worried about for a long time, even though I didn't give up eating, sleeping or chasing cats and birds because of worry.

One day while on the beach with Daddy Jim, I figured it out. While running on the beach, I was taking about sixteen steps to Jim's one large step (really eight on each set of legs—front and back). That alone is wearing me down sixteen times faster than Daddy Jim. And when I eat, I gulp down my food, and I'm done with it shortly after I smell it (probably ten times faster than Daddy Jim). That's just my nature. And Jim and others like "3d 🐾", and Dogma mince over their food always taking their time and relaxing. I get things done in a hurry, and I think it all balances out. And, I sleep a lot more than they do, so it works out to that seven-to-one ratio. And the I remembered a lesson I learned from my little nun sister, Sister Robert, before they hauled her off to the convent. She told me of a wonderful life to come after this one in a place called Heaven. Sooo, it seems that I'll get there before any of them, especially with the influence my sister must surely have with the Mother Superior, and perhaps with some of the other higher-ups by this time. I decided to quit worrying about that one/seven thing and get back to enjoying life by eating, sleeping, chasing cats, and continuing to try to learn to fly so I can catch a seagull.

The Dachshund Diet

Not long after I figured out the reasoning of the one/seven ratio and was able to deal with it, another much more miserable catastrophe struck! And this time it came again from that wretch, the Vet. Jim took me in for a tooth cleaning. The guy always zapped me with a needle and put me out while he worked on my teeth. He told Daddy Jim that this was necessary to make me relax so that he could do a better job. I knew better, of course. He put me out to keep me from biting him while he did that better job!

When I came out from under the influence of that danged needle (admittedly with cleaner and whiter teeth), he told Jim that I was two pounds overweight, and that it would be a good idea for me to lose that extra weight as soon as possible. He pointed out that two pounds overweight on me was like having twenty pounds of extra weight on Daddy Jim or "3d ❤." I'll never understand how they come up with these ratios, but here again was a one/ten ratio, but this time in my favor. If I had to lose twenty pounds. I'd be well, uh, dead!

I didn't think too much about the weight loss matter until that evening when Daddy Jim prepared my science diet dinner. Instead of the usual half can that I'd become accustomed to, my ration had been cut to one-third can. And worse yet, there were no nibbles from Jim's pork chop after he had finished his dinner. I went to bed hungry, hating that Vet even more than ever, and I was a little peeved with Jim for even listening to him. He seemed to be having just too much influence over my life. I dreamed about that Vet that night. He had horns and a long tail with a hook on it.

The next morning was even worse. Instead of the usual five or six biscuits I usually had, my ration had been reduced to only two! And when we arrived at Jim's office, I found that the usual generosity of the office staff had been obliterated too. The same thing from all of them as I sniffed at their desk drawers, "Sorry, Isabella, no more cookies." I felt like the dog in Old Mother Hubbard's rhyme where the cupboard was always bare when she went "to get her poor dog a bone."

It wasn't but a few days until I learned that Jim was off on another journey and that I would be spending time with Dogma and "3d 🐾" while he was away. I was quite sure that "3d 🐾" would be his usual generous self and lay out the grub when I asked for it. But no such luck! Jim had brought along the science diet stuff with strict instructions about my daily allowance.

I pouted, of course, and put on a sad face, and continued to hate the Vet, even though I was able to notice a slight decrease in my waistline. And I was getting used to it. I didn't seem as hungry, even on this starvation diet! And while "3d 🐾" was considering my situation, and was admiring my slimmer waistline, he decided that if my diet worked for me, then something similar should work for him. He admitted to being twenty pounds overweight! Since he didn't enjoy my science diet, he adapted my diet to his own needs, and thus was born "The Dachshund Diet." Here is how it worked for "3d 🐾":

For breakfast: one small dish of oatmeal or other unsweetened cereal with skim milk and one cup of coffee or decaff.

For lunch: One can of "Slim Fast" or other diet drink with vitamins and minerals necessary for healthy living. (This is a substitute for my science diet which has the vitamins and minerals necessary for MY healthy living.)

Before dinner: One martini or other cocktail instead of the usual three or four that he had grown accustomed to, accompanied by hors d'oeuvres such as carrot sticks or celery or a raw mushroom. "3d 🐾" let me join him for cocktails, but I've never been able to stand booze. I did, however learn to eat carrots and celery, even though I felt as though it was like letting the moon shine on my face!

For dinner; Vegetables, vegetables, vegetables, accompanied by a small piece of lean meat, and no dessert other than yogurt, a non-fat fruit bar, or a piece of fresh fruit.

"3d 🐾" and I both suffered for about a week, and then the Dachshund Diet began to work. I lost my two pounds faster than he lost his twenty, but this was one ratio that seemed to be in my favor. I'm now two pounds lighter, and I don't really miss the extra intake to which I'd grown accustomed. "3d 🐾" dropped his twenty pounds and is living proof that the Dachshund Diet really does get results. He is sticking to the diet and maintaining his weight. (I think he sneaks an extra cocktail now and then.)

Jim is proud of me, and Dogma is proud of "3d 🐾", and I've almost gotten over my dislike for that wretched Vet.

Jail Time

Like most law abiding citizens, I never dreamed that one day I'd end up in the hoosegow, but one day I did just that, and really through no fault of my own. It happened like this:

Daddy Jim received a call from a former college roommate who was going to be on a business trip from New York to the West Coast. Since they had not seen each other for years, Jim urged him to come to Carmel and spend a few days with us. The guy's name was Durwood, and he arrived with bag and baggage INCLUDING A DAWG!!!!!

The dog was a big rascal, and even though friendly, I disliked him from the beginning. His name was Ralph. He wanted to sleep in my bed. He wanted to eat out of my dish, even though Durwood had brought his own for him. He slobbered. He stole my ball and several of my other favorite toys. And worst of all, I had to share Daddy Jim with the two of them.

Some folks don't realize that jealousy is a natural instinct with us Dachshunds. Instead of holding me on his lap and petting me while we watched T.V. in the evening, Daddy Jim talked to Durwood and patted Ralph on the head, giving me only the slightest of attention.

One afternoon, Durwood wanted to see our quaint little town, so the two of them went out and took the Dawg with them. I guess I should have been grateful that they decided to leave me at home alone, but, I wasn't grateful at all. As a matter of fact I was furious. One might say that I was really "weedled" off!!!

Daddy Jim and I often walked to our office, it was only three blocks away, and I knew the way. Sometimes Jim would even let me go without a leash, even though our town has a leash law (except on the beach). Thinking quickly, I decided to dig under the fence and go to the office, since I was rather certain I'd find them there, and everyone would think "how cute." If Jim and his guests were not there, I was certain members of the staff would be, and they could entertain me until Daddy Jim showed up. The dig out was rather easy. And soon I was on my way to town without leash, without tags, but with a determined mind.

Along the way several ladies stopped to admire me and pet me; I just wagged my tail and enjoyed the attention, and went on my way to our office. Then, a very nice lady pulled up in a little truck and side parked. She was very nice and came over to pet me. She even gave me a cookie. I ate it while she petted, and then figured that I would once again be on my way. But suddenly I found myself in her arms and then, even more suddenly, I was in the back of her little truck in a CAGE. Very soon I was in a part of town I had never seen. I was whisked into a large room with several cages, all containing animals, and I realized to my horror that I was in jail.

Well to say the least, I was petrified. What had I done wrong? Was this a life sentence? Was I on death row? How could Daddy Jim ever find me, and even if he did find me would they let him take me home? How could I end up in jail when all I had done was walk along the streets looking for Daddy Jim? Then I figured it out!! They thought that I was a street walker—a prostitute!!! Yipes!!!

It seemed that I was in jail for a very long time, and I am sure that I was there for overnight, since they fed me dinner. Then I slept for a little while, and when I awoke it was light and they fed me something for breakfast. But one day in Dachshund time is like one week.

That afternoon, while still grieving inwardly, the door to the room opened, and I heard the jailer say, "Well, come on and have a look; I believe we may have her." I felt my heart leap with joy. The jailer continued, "But you'll have to prove that she is yours since she had no collar or tag."

Daddy Jim entered the room. I screamed. They opened the door to my cage and Jim picked me up. I was so glad to see him that I couldn't stop crying, and his arms were wet since I just couldn't help weedling all over him. I gave him one of my slurpies across the mouth, and saw that he too was crying with joy.

"Well," said the jailer, "there is no doubt that you two belong together. You may take her after you pay your fine of thirty-five dollars."

"Gladly," said Daddy Jim, and he did. We went outside, got in our little red convertible and went home. Durwood was gone; the Dawg was gone, I had my dish, my bed, my toys, and best of all I had Daddy Jim all to myself. And, I've learned my lesson. I'll never ever go out again all by myself.

After Daddy Jim got over being happy about having me back, he picked me up, put me on his lap, looked me in the eyes and said, "Now see here, Isabella, it cost me thirty-five dollars to get you out of the pound, and you received no punishment at all for running away, and walking downtown alone and without identification. They were very lenient with you, but they punished me with a fine. Therefore, young lady, I'm going to sentence you myself to two days of community service." And he didn't elaborate.

He put me down and went outside leaving me to worry about what kind of "community service" he might have in mind. I couldn't deliver Meals on Wheels 'cause I can't drive without a lap to sit on and someone to turn the steering wheel. I can't visit the elderly and shut-ins in nursing homes 'cause I've never had the training to be a therapy canine. I just could not imagine what kind of "community service" I could possibly do. But the answer was soon in coming.

Third Paw Rings a Bell

The next morning, right after my breakfast, "3d 🐾" arrived with a new Christmas collar for me. It was red velvet with little tufts of white, and between each tuft was a little silver bell that jingled when I had it on and moved my head. Wearing it made me look even cuter than usual. "3d 🐾" said that for the past several years he had been a volunteer at Christmastime for the Salvation Army. He took a two-hour shift of ringing the bell so as to "keep the pot boiling"—(their way of raising money). This year he had signed up for two days, and he wanted to take me with him, to show me off, and perhaps, because of me, increase the intake. I was overjoyed, and Daddy Jim agreed that this would serve as my two days of "community service."

We arrived at our post at two o'clock in the afternoon outside a drugstore where there was a lot of foot traffic. "3d 🐾" brought along a stool and a cushion for me to sit on while he rang the bell. We were an immediate success. People would walk by, hear the bell, greet. "3d 🐾" see me and want to pet me. I loved it. After petting me and often getting a slurpy kiss on the hand they would turn to the bucket and "3d 🐾" and give generously. They really kept that pot boiling. Poor "3d 🐾" was always tired from ringing the bell at the end of our two-hour shifts, but not me. He had to stand and ring, and all I had to do was sit and look cute. I hope he'll let me do "community service" with him again next year. It was a wonderful experience, and being right in the Holiday Season, made me want to say "Happy Holidays" to everyone. Even that Vet!